KING
PONG

'King Pong'
An original concept by Clare Helen Welsh
© Clare Helen Welsh

Illustrated by Kelly Breemer

Published by MAVERICK ARTS PUBLISHING LTD
Studio 3A, City Business Centre, 6 Brighton Road,
Horsham, West Sussex, RH13 5BB
© Maverick Arts Publishing Limited January 2019
+44 (0)1403 256941

A CIP catalogue record for this book is available at the British Library.

ISBN 978-1-84886-403-0

www.maverickbooks.co.uk

This book is rated as: Gold Band (Guided Reading)

KING PONG

By **Clare Helen Welsh**

Illustrated by **Kelly Breemer**

Chapter 1

In a hot, green jungle a long, long way from here, lived a gorilla.

He had kind eyes and his body was covered in jet black hair, except his back which was spattered with silver. He was stronger and braver than any other gorilla before him. He was stronger and braver than any other animal in the whole of the jungle!

But he was also smelly, which was why they
called him... King Pong!

"Watch out, here comes Pong!" the colourful parrots cawed.

"Knot your trunks and take cover!" the jolly elephants trumpeted.

"Eurgh! He smells worse than he did yesterday," the lazy crocodiles complained.

"If that's even possible!"

But King Pong didn't know his armpits smelt
like week old bananas... and no one told him.
Not even the monkeys dangling in the trees.

He didn't know his feet smelt like dung
balls... and no one explained.

Not even the snakes slithering across the floor.

He didn't know his fur smelt worse than anything anyone had ever smelt before. And no one mentioned it, not even the fruit flies.

All the animals loved King Pong and no one wanted to hurt his feelings. So King Pong merrily went about his day, chasing ants and finding leaves to make nests with.

Chapter 2

But one sunny, summer's day, King Pong's stink became unbearable! The jungle air was hot and sticky and there was no breeze to blow away bad smells. Whilst King Pong napped, the jungle animals gathered in a clearing for an emergency meeting.

"When was the last time that big, hairy lump had a wash?" they asked each other.

But that was precisely King Pong's problem. He didn't wash! Not even on Sundays. Not even on his birthday. Not ever!

"He's so strong he rescued Rhino with one hand!" explained Elephant. "But he's too scared to paddle in a puddle."

"He's so brave he freed Falcon with his eyes shut!" said Giraffe. "But he's too scared to dip his toe in water."

"He's so kind he saved Snake even when he was really tired!" said Hippo. "But a drop of rain sends him into a panic!"

King Pong's stink was putting whole herds of animals off their food! It was stinging the baby animals' eyes too! "Wahhh! Wahhh! Wahhh!" they cried.

The animals needed to do something... and quick!

Chapter 3

King Pong woke up from his relaxing nap and went for a stroll by the water.

"It's now or never," the animals thought.

"What a hot day," said Elephant washing her trunk, "Why don't you take a paddle in the pool?"

King Pong shivered and shuddered at the thought. "I- I can't! It's too wet!" he said.

"Why don't you just float a little on the surface?" said Crocodile relaxing on his back.

King Pong's knuckles trembled and his teeth chattered. "N- n- no way! It's too cold!" he said.

"Nonsense! It's lovely and warm," said Hippo wallowing in the shallows.

"Hold your breath and dive in!"

But...

"...I'm too scared!" wailed King Pong backing away.

The animals didn't want to make King Pong upset but they couldn't stand his stink any longer. They wanted to help their friend overcome his fear too. He was always helping others after all.

So whilst King Pong was having his second nap of the day, the animals called another emergency meeting.

Chapter 4

The animals thought long and hard about ways to help King Pong. But the stink was getting to them and no one could agree.

"We can't tell him! He'll be upset!" the colourful parrots cawed.

"We can't push him in. He'll be even more scared!" the jolly elephants trumpeted.

"We should just mind our own business!" the lazy crocodiles suggested, which was easy for them to say. They could hold their breath underwater for hours!

Just at that moment a terrifying sound echoed through the jungle.

"Help! Help! Someone HELP!"

It was so loud and so terrifying it woke King Pong from his nap!

It was Giraffe. She was deep in the middle of the water and she was in trouble!

Elephant couldn't rescue her. She wasn't brave enough. Crocodile couldn't rescue her. He wasn't strong enough. Hippo couldn't rescue her. Where was Hippo?

There was only one animal strong and brave and courageous enough. But was he up to the job?

King Pong jumped down from his nest and charged towards the water.

"Ooo! Ooo! Ahhh! Ahhh!" he called to let the others know he was on his way.

But he stopped at once when he saw the problem. He wanted to help. He really did.

"I- I can't. Not water... someone else will have to go," he said shaking his head.

But then Giraffe called out again, "Help us, please! It's not just me! It's Gemma too!"

That's when King Pong realised Giraffe wasn't on her own.

Chapter 5

When King Pong saw that Gemma, Giraffe's calf, was in trouble too he didn't hesitate. He took a long, deep breath and...

SPLASH!

He swam! All the way towards his friends. The giraffes were stuck to something dark and round and it was pulling them under! But what was it?!

King Pong ducked his head beneath the water to find out.

That's when he worked out what was really going on. The dark and round something was Hippo! And he wasn't pulling them under... he was holding them up!

King Pong came up for air. "Hippo?" he cried. "What are you doing here?"

Although he already knew the answer to that. Giraffe and her calf were clapping and cheering. All of the other animals were grinning widely too.

Then King Pong realised something else. The water wasn't cold and scary. It was warm and refreshing and fun.

"Well done," said Elephant.

"Hooray," said Crocodile.

"You did it!" said Hippo and the giraffes.

When King Pong eventually got out of the water, he was the cleanest he had ever been! All the jungle animals breathed a huge, fresh, sigh of relief.

"Does that mean I can have a new nickname now?" he asked.

"What do you mean?" pretended Elephant.

"What are you talking about?" shuffled Giraffe.

"I think he knows," whispered Hippo.

"I know you call me King Pong," he said

looking glumly at the ground.

Suddenly all the animals felt a bit bad. "We're sorry," they said.

"It's ok, you helped me find the courage to go into the water," King Pong said with a smile. "I couldn't have done it without you."

"Hip, hip hooray for King Splash!" the animals cheered.

In a hot, green jungle a long, long way from here, lived a gorilla. He was stronger, braver and cleaner than any other animal ever before him. And now...

"OOO! OOO! AHHH! AHHH!"

...he loved the water!

But maybe a little too much.

SPLASH!

The End

Book Bands for Guided Reading

The Institute of Education book banding system is a scale of colours that reflects the various levels of reading difficulty. The bands are assigned by taking into account the content, the language style, the layout and phonics. Word, phrase and sentence level work is also taken into consideration.

Maverick Early Readers are a bright, attractive range of books covering the pink to white bands. All of these books have been book banded for guided reading to the industry standard and edited by a leading educational consultant.

Pink
Red
Yellow
Blue
Green
Orange
Turquoise
Purple
Gold
White

To view the whole Maverick Readers scheme, visit our website at
www.maverickearlyreaders.com

Or scan the QR code above to view our scheme instantly!